T0198773

The WIZARD LOST IN TIME

GRACE TUTTLE

Balboa Press books may be ordered through booksellers or by contacting:

Balboa Press
A Division of Hay House
1663 Liberty Drive
Bloomington, IN 47403
www.balboapress.com
844-682-1282

ISBN: 979-8-7652-3297-2 (sc)
ISBN: 979-8-7652-3298-9 (e)

Print information available on the last page.

Balboa Press rev. date: 10/19/2022

BALBOA.PRESS
A DIVISION OF HAY HOUSE

Wizards lost in time .by

Grace Tuttle

My Grandfather went back in time to explore the 1800 but that was when my mother was gril . my Grandmother he went with his zack who happens to be a alline . I saw a lot of photos of him when my mother was there when she taught her magic . They used to travel with the alien family all thim to 1976 to see a lot of aliens come to earth, nice and friendly. We hide them and make them look human or have them live where there are giant unicorns. My friend wants to see a real live one candy . I'm getting off track but this year I am making a plan to rescue my grandfather, mom and grandmother.

It's August fifth and I have to go back to magic school soon but this year I'm determined to get back my grandfather .

"Mother, look over here I have found a looking glass that's still glowing." Said Jill

"Your grandfather was lost years ago his we still care about him and we still get mail though the chimney."said Jane jill's mom

"I know there is a lot of mail and thousands of letters saying help!" said the daughter .

"Yes but how can I survive after all these years of being gone? It's been two years séance he's been gone."

"Yes but wizards and witches can live longer than normal people . Also we can find him. He left a journal that might tell us where and how disappeared. This last letter there is a small image of him in the background that looks like the 1800."

"Yes and we can help him."

"Just how can you do that if you or I have never tried this magic before . The magic he was doing was very advanced for a young lady or even me ." You are twelve years old and you still have a lot of school until you know what you are doing . I'll try to get people at wizard elders to help."

"Jemil Fannie Kroon, not another word about it ! "said Jane Jill's mom. " Yes mother," said Jill.

A cat came up to her and started to purr and looked up to her face and it kept trying to cheer her up. It was the end of summer . Then all of the blue fireplace started to crackle. Help me a voice from it came. She took a look at the fire and she saw a carriage boat, and people in Slaves looked away in some of the cages . all witch where busted wide open. He was fighting another wizard . in a few minutes the flam were gone and she could no longer see or hear anything anymore.

At once she knew that her Grandfather was alive and while in the past some where. All she one fine day he was gone it was a Friday afternoon she was at school and her parents had came home he was gone there was just one note. On a pillow in his bedroom it said i'll be back soon to love Grandfather. It was also her fist day of school. That was also two year ago .

She went up to the top of the house where they where not aloud to go. That where Howards Kroon books of spells and old maps. She was looking around for clues to what was her Grandfather doing ? the cat had followed her up top it let out a meow .

"Oh that is you Jim the cat." shush I'm breaking the house rule of being up here we are going to get caught. In the corner stood and old elf owl. It was sleeping because it would only be awake at night. The house has been in their family for generation. It was dark and hard to see. It was a big house with nice few and both a front and back garden

"Jemil, it's almost time for you to go to the first day of school." Where are you?"

"I'm in my room," she said, trying not to get caught."

"No, I'm in your room ." Now where are you ? said her mother.

I pet the cat and set in up room . I've been searching upstairs where my grandfather lived and I found a recording journal. I think it will be the key to find what happen and where I need to go to find my lost grandfather . I'll get my friends to help me get my grandfather .

She came quietly down stairs and began to get ready for magic school grabbing her flying broom and magic bag,an wond, she hugged her mom goodbye.

"Mom, I know that I can do this, just give me a chance to find him.

"No, traveling back in time is not safe where you can get hurt or losts I don't want that to happen to you."

"Ok i won't go she said with a sad look on face while looking down at the floor shuffling her feet."

"Promise me you won't go."

"Ok I promise I won't go and try to save my grandfather." She said this while looking up at her mother and said it with a more convening voice than before.

She uses her wone to make magic fog so no one could see her flying to a school of magic . She came to the school just in time . She landed in front of the school and met up with her friends Candy, Fred and an old friend the family Ben who was an alien. The alien knew the family since 1978. He and the grandfather had always gone different adverts together back in the past to different plants. They have always gone back alright but this time when my GrandFather has gone to the past with ben bother this time they didn't come back.

I'm walking over to my friends to ask for help in getting my grandfather back home when the professor Glenmore walked up.

Hello students of magic ? This way to position the class is about to start." said professor Glenmore.

"Wait, my grandfather has been gone for a long time from my life.

Can you please help go and find him?

I know he's still alive. I heard his voice just this morning.

Ok we can help you. Said Candy

Yes we'll all help you with a task like that you need good friends to help you. They did not know what they would find they know it would find in the 1800 but they did know that they didn't want Jill to go there alone . they took out their wons and used the journal as a guide to go back to the past . she had it out of the bag she was carrying it in. They worked together to make a time pratal using a magic spell .

They were noticed as soons they got into 1800 .

"Look witches, wizards ahh a big blue thing they have with them get them all they are not one of us." said a voice

They were outside standing in the middle of England rear some houses and apartments in the 1800 wearing 21st clothes on and Ben the alien stood out because of his blue skin.

"We better get out of here before they form a big mob." Said Fred.

I know a place where we can go to the dancing unicorn, a magic pub and inn. Owned by an old friend of mine. Said professor Glenmore.

They then took off on brooms which they took with them on entering the 1800. Following Mr Glenmore to a safe place .

They got the place about the middle of the day when they came of plan to rescue her grandfather from a big table in the pub. The owner was a sixteen feet giant friendly and his name is John.

He served them drinks and foods and gave them a map of England .

You should stay here for the night where hoping fully you be safe said James

"There are lots of wizards also dancing to unicorns . "said Fred.

Yes this safe place from all the bad wizards there is magic protecting this place at all times .

Petter Glenmore you just an young wizard doing this time period you need to hide from you or it might change everything in present time you need to get back to the present as soon as find her grandfather there lots of dark wizards who stop of nothing not to change anything slavory, and they been after me and you for years up to this point we are going to have revolution that will take away their its your plan to stop them and to help with free the slaves in England . said James who is a gait.

The group meeting tonight I believe your grandfather got caught by those wizards and is in jail . said James .

Ok so how do I avoid two of me being here at the same time ? said Petter Glenmore

Just go upstairs in the inn part of the dancing unicorn .

On the table in the bup where they are eating there wase a picture of my grandfather standing by ufo and aline ben's bother giving themselves up to a group of angry mob . The alien was in slave chains

"Why didn't he fight back ?" said Jill

My guess he didn't want to hurt the people that's my bother and your grandfather way he might try to escape them out there said Ben the aline

"blasting with strong magic or even using an alien strength and fighting any one is not his still he is more a lover than a fighter. Said Ben

Let's stay here for the night, get some rest and keep rescuing them . said Ben

"Yes you need to learn how to defend yourself against the dark wizard and witches doing this time period," said Mr Glenmore

"We all have to face them at one point."

"I would like to thank you all for coming here with me and risking everything . said Jill

Your welcome we all friends here we all care a great deal about you Jill. said Candy

Ok lights out said the giant time for bed. It is eight at night. They went up stairs to their own separate rooms .

The giant hooked them up with nice rooms with no charger based on the fact that James got help from my family and professor Gelmore helped him buy the pub.

We woke inside the dancing uncion we knew where my Grandfather was and how to get him out was going to be difficult . She began to get dressed. There was a nice dress laid out for her. It has such a nice red color. The dress was also an old fatsation you had to pull strings in the back for you to wear it.

She got ready and dressed then she started to look for her friends . she thought maybe she could text her friends to get them all in one group but no could charge their cell phones . you could not contact your friends in minutes if lost or hurt . If you want to find somewhere you need to go you just have to read a map . I hope that doesn't happen to us.

"Good morning Jill how did you sleep ?""

"Morning Candy I slept ok ." said Jill

"You know what i found no way to plug in my cell phone and they want us to wear thighs that you have put on so we blend in to the croud so you don't get spotted by 1800 wizards or people who hate witches for using magic and wanted to burn them to stake said Candy

"Let's go down stairs. " siad Jill

Hopefully everyone is already up and dress in 1800 clothes so we can try to blend in,.said Candy

'How would that work for Ben who is an alien ?"

They went down stairs and luckily every one was all gather in dining area waiting for them to come down stairs .

"Good morning ladies come down stairs. We have a plan now that we need to put into action . said Mr Glenmore

The giant will act as a distraction he will make sure everything and everyone will be chasing him. While we all use a spell to make us look like a mist or big group of clouds in the sky.

We know from the newspaper where they have them in jail but we are going to break them out and then go back to the year 2022. Said Mr Gelnmore .

They go out the back exit w\hil the giant goes out the front waving a club about

Saying words like come and get me making a thug sioud with his club.

We start to take off on the brooms Ben shared my broom,

Why were we in clouds in the sky on the way to bust out my grandfather. We were attacked by what looked like a dark cloud black and lighting in the clouds and they were moving right to us .

"Kill them said a voice in the dark clouds ;

"Be quiet Simon just do it, kill them all make them fall down dead.

We use a spell to defend ourselves, which makes it seem to work .

Then the alien ben makes a big blast of shield using his attana and hands it was too big we separated after the big blast

t was now dark again . we could not see and the group of us was that was together nervous and sacred A slave that was in changes and carring a lightern came up to the ladies and then he spoke to them. You can hear the chain clang, clang and they saw how he walked slowly because of the chains. When the slave go close to them he intorduce him self to the ladies

"Hello there you look lost. My name is Christpher follow me and let's take you to my master. She can help you."

"Ok trying to hide their wons in their purses and also the brooms behind their back. See witches in this time period where all conder evil. Even though some were good. They didn't want to be caught by any one or make it seem that from a different time period they might arrest them for being witches. So they were trying to blend in as much as possible .

They were relieved when they knew they could trust him. After all, he was bound. Their first thought was feeling sad for him. They decided to say something back .

"Hi my name is Jill, this candy and Liza."said Jill

Nice evening. Said Jill

"Let me take you too my master she a nice lady " said Christopher

They follow him back to where he worked as an slave . it was a nice big house with a front garden.

They ring the doorbell and women yong opens the door

"Hello my name is Ms Marland"

"I'm one of the few humans like magic and want to free all the slaves ." said Ms Marland

There is something I think you should see in the back garden. She was holding a remote something from 2022. We walked back with her. It was me,Candy and Liza that came with us. We walked to the back of the garden and saw our way home and out of this mess a ufo.

"This what they came in . " said Candy

Ms .Marland opens the ufo with the remote . they get into the ufo lucky there was instruction in the ufo . They locate every one and bembem them aboard the UFO and use it to go back to the president's time .

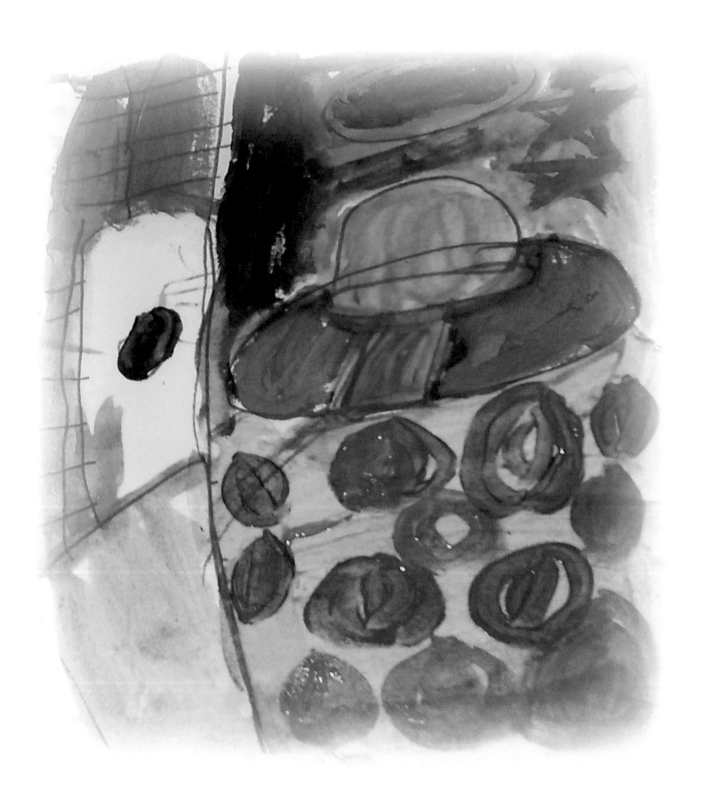

Everyone is back and I'm spending a lot of time with my grandfather. People have lots of questions . They want to know how the 1800 was . it was tough to get back thankfully there is an alien spaceship in Ms Marland's back yard . We use that to get back home.

I was glad to have my cat and grandmother and grandfather make up for lost time. It was a miracle we made it back in one piece.

I'm hope us bring a slave to the 21 centery would cause any trouble for us here .

Right now we are celebrating our happy return the whole school and some other wizards are doing the limbo rock .

Unbelievable aline in middle of autortorman doing the limbo rock with Fred, my mom, father, and bunch of the students .

Looking forward to a great rest of the school year its now September the 4th and on monday we have to a test on spells but for now party .

THE END.

Printed in the United States
by Baker & Taylor Publisher Services